GIANTS of RAP and HIP-HOP

CARDI B

Stuart A. Kallen

San Diego, CA

© 2020 ReferencePoint Press, Inc.
Printed in the United States

For more information, contact:
ReferencePoint Press, Inc.
PO Box 27779
San Diego, CA 92198
www.ReferencePointPress.com

ALL RIGHTS RESERVED.
No part of this work covered by the copyright hereon may be reproduced or used in any form or by any means—graphic, electronic, or mechanical, including photocopying, recording, taping, web distribution, or information storage retrieval systems—without the written permission of the publisher.

LIBRARY OF CONGRESS CATALOGING-IN-PUBLICATION DATA

Name: Kallen, Stuart A., 1955– author.
Title: Cardi B/by Stuart A. Kallen.
Description: San Diego: ReferencePoint Press, 2019. | Series: Giants of Rap and Hip-Hop | Includes bibliographical references and index.
Identifiers: LCCN 2019041303 (print) | LCCN 2019041304 (ebook) | ISBN 9781682827758 (library binding) | ISBN 9781682827765 (ebook)
Subjects: LCSH: Cardi B, 1992—Juvenile literature. | Rap musicians—United States—Biography—Juvenile literature.
Classification: LCC ML3930.C255 K35 2019 (print) | LCC ML3930.C255 (ebook) | DDC 782.421649092 [B]—dc23
LC record available at https://lccn.loc.gov/2019041303
LC ebook record available at https://lccn.loc.gov/2019041304

Introduction 4
Empowered and Empowering

Chapter One 7
Born in the Bronx

Chapter Two 18
Building a Following

Chapter Three 29
The Hottest Thing in Hip-Hop

Chapter Four 40
Hip-Hop's Reigning Queen

Source Notes 52
Important Events in the Life of Cardi B 56
For More Information 57
Index 58
Picture Credits 63
About the Author 64

EMPOWERED AND EMPOWERING

In October 2018 music journalist Vanessa Grigoriadis called Cardi B the "new princess of hip-hop"[1] in a feature article in *Rolling Stone* magazine. At the time, the twenty-five-year-old hip-hop princess from the Bronx, New York, was riding a wild trajectory to international stardom that most rappers could barely imagine. Cardi B's debut single, "Bodak Yellow (Money Moves)," hit number one in July 2017. In the year that followed, Cardi married rap star Offset; recorded her breakout album, *Invasion of Privacy*; and gave birth to a daughter named Kulture Kiari Cephus.

Invasion of Privacy set an Apple Music record for the most first-week streams by a female artist. The double-platinum album (with sales over 2 million) won the Grammy for Best Rap Album. Cardi also racked up seven *Billboard* music awards and nine Black Entertainment Television (BET) Hip Hop Awards. The singles from *Invasion of Privacy* set two Guinness world records: Cardi B holds the record for the most simultaneous *Billboard* Hot 100 entries by a female and the most simultaneous *Billboard* Hot R&B/Hip-Hop top-ten entries by a female in one week. These accomplishments put newcomer Cardi B in front of established superstars like Beyoncé and Nicki Minaj.

Smarts, Talent, and Drive

With a net worth of over $12 million in 2019, some might call Cardi B an overnight success. But her trip to the top in hip-hop was not always easy. As a student, she showed both smarts and talent—excelling in politics and history in college while developing a good singing voice. But Cardi was trapped in a bad relationship with nowhere to go. She began working as a stripper so she could gain her independence.

Cardi B had drive and ambition. In 2015 she developed a large social media following on Instagram. She taught herself to rap and went on to record two mixtapes of original music. This move led to a role on the VH1 reality show *Love & Hip-Hop: New York*. And while she was five months pregnant, she spent every day in the studio recording *Invasion of Privacy*. As Craig Kallman, the chief executive officer of Atlantic Records, says, "She was a ferocious worker, unreal. I think she wanted to show women around the world that you can have it all. And I think she's showing that."[2]

Cardi B performs at the Music Midtown festival in Atlanta in 2019. She has become one of the most successful female rappers of her time.

Breaking Rules, Busting Down Doors

Cardi B's hot rap lyrics, or *bars* in hip-hop slang, are sometimes vulgar and controversial. But her astounding success in a male-dominated genre proves she has few equals. In this often-misogynistic field, Cardi is an outspoken feminist: "Being a feminist is real simple; it's that a woman can do things the same as a man. . . . Anything a man can do, I can do. I can finesse, I can hustle. . . . I was [at the] top of the charts. I'm a woman and I did that. I do feel equal to a man."[3]

> "Being a feminist is real simple. . . . Anything a man can do, I can do. I can finesse, I can hustle."[3]
>
> —Cardi B

Cardi B says she understands that some people are frightened by an influential, rule-breaking black woman such as herself. But she is not afraid to stand up for her beliefs—whether she is criticizing the president or endorsing a politician. As Cardi explains, "I love political science. . . . I love government. I'm obsessed with presidents. I'm obsessed to know how the system works. . . . I'm always watching the news. . . . [I'm] concerned about it because [I'm] a citizen of America . . . a citizen of the world."[4]

Cardi B sometimes jokes about running for president, but she would have to be thirty-five years old to do so. Until that day in 2027, Cardi can express herself to 49 million Instagram followers who laugh at her jokes, imitate her fashions, buy her records, and swoon over Kulture Kiari's baby pictures.

Cardi B followed a path to hip-hop stardom blazed by raw and aggressive female rappers like Lil' Kim, Nicki Minaj, and Foxy Brown. She can spit out a staccato flow of twisted words and bent phrases with the best of them. And in doing so, she became the crown princess of hip-hop. By being herself, Cardi B has become a rap icon while busting down doors for other women who hope the hip-hop spotlight will shine on them one day.

BORN IN THE BRONX

Cardi B was born Belcalis Marlenis Almánzar in the Bronx borough of New York City on October 11, 1992. Her father, Carlos Almánzar, immigrated to New York from the Dominican Republic and found work as a taxi driver. Cardi's mother, who has African and Spanish heritage, was born in the Republic of Trinidad and Tobago; she worked as a cashier. Although Cardi will rap about every subject—from working as a stripper to the most intimate details of her personal life—she refuses to reveal her mother's name in order to protect her identity. Cardi B has a younger sister, Hennessy Carolina Almánzar, who was born in 1995. Soon after Hennessy was born, their parents divorced. Their mother eventually remarried and Cardi and Hennessy grew up with a stepfather, but they also saw their father on a regular basis.

It was Carlos who both directly and indirectly influenced the naming of his daughters. According to Hennessy, Carlos named her after his favorite brand of French cognac. At some point in their childhood, friends picked up on the liquor theme and began calling Belcalis by the nickname Bacardi (after a brand of Cuban rum). As Cardi explains, "My sister's name is Hennessy, so everybody used to be like 'Bacardi' to me. Then I shortened it to Cardi B. The 'B' stands for whatever, depending on the day . . . beautiful or bully. . . . No one calls me Belcalis except for my family, my mother and my daddy."[5]

While Cardi went on to become a rap superstar, Hennessy studied at the Fashion Institute of Technology in New York City. Known for her unusual fashion sense, Hennessy was working to launch her own clothing line in 2019.

CHAPTER ONE

A Tough Neighborhood

Cardi and her family lived in Highbridge, a Latino neighborhood in the South Bronx. Because their mother worked two jobs, Cardi and Hennessy often lived with their grandmother, Esperanza Almánzar, in Manhattan's Washington Heights neighborhood. Although Cardi maintains a close relationship with Esperanza, she blames her grandmother for her strong accent. Cardi's parents both spoke Spanish; her father is not fluent in English, and Cardi says her mother speaks "broken" English. Cardi's first language was Spanish, and though she learned to speak English fluently as a young girl, she has a slight Spanish accent. Added to that is the strong New York accent she picked up from her grandmother. This accent is noted for its rounded vowels and elongated consonants, as Cardi explains: "I don't got the best English in the world. . . . I will say, 'turning you awhn,' not 'turning you on.'. . . [Or I'll say] get awhff me. . . . It's a really bad pet peeve of mine. I can't help it."[6]

Washington Heights was viewed as a better neighborhood than the South Bronx. Even though the South Bronx was undergoing extensive renovation during the second half of the 1990s, it was still considered a tough area with a legacy of poverty and violence. Cardi went to school in Washington Heights until she was eleven. When she started sixth grade in the South Bronx, she says she was unaccustomed to how much everyone cursed. And all the girls wanted to fight her. By the time she was in middle school, Cardi says she just accepted that this was normal—she had to defend herself every day at school.

> "I don't got the best English in the world. . . . It's a really bad pet peeve of mine."[6]
>
> —Cardi B

Cardi's Strict Mom

Cardi was an eyewitness to violence when she was thirteen. She was driving in a van with Hennessy and her father when a man fell in front of the vehicle. Cardi screamed that her father had hit the man. But when they got out of the van to help him, they discov-

Cardi (left) poses with her younger sister, Hennessy (right), at the 60th Grammy Awards in 2018. Hennessy is a fashion designer.

ered he had been shot in the head—apparently a victim of gang violence. Cardi's takeaway from the shooting incident was not what might be expected. Rather than thinking she should avoid gangs, she saw the man's death as just another normal part of daily life. She also noticed that the most popular kids in her school were gang members, and she wanted to hang out with them.

Cardi was attracted to gangs because she believed they might provide a sense of security that was lacking at home. She saw her mother working extremely hard at two jobs, but her family continued to struggle. This made her realize early on that life could be full of disappointments. As Cardi said in 2016, "You know when you're a kid, it's like, 'Oh my god, I want to be an astronaut!' or like 'Oh my gosh, I want to be an actor.' But then when you're in high school reality kicks in."[7]

Cardi's reality included a very stern mother who severely limited her social life—including prohibiting her daughter from going on sleepovers with friends. And Cardi was afraid to disobey, saying she was always more afraid of her mom than the gangbangers at school. While Cardi's mom imposed restrictions to keep her daughter from joining a gang, she had another reason to be protective: Cardi's health was fragile. She suffered from chronic asthma; after a severe attack, she might end up in the hospital for two weeks or more. At home, Cardi used a breathing apparatus called a nebulizer machine, which delivered medicine to her lungs to help her breathe. However, the medicine gave her tremors. Cardi later recalled, "My mom used to cry a lot be-

Cardi grew up in the South Bronx (pictured in the 1990s) in New York City. The area was impoverished and had a high crime rate.

cause she used to be scared that I would fall asleep and die of an asthma attack. . . . People used to tell my mom, 'She's not going to make it.'"[8]

When laid up after an asthma attack, Cardi had plenty of time to watch television. Her favorite show was *That's So Raven*, which featured an African American teenager, Raven Baxter, who had psychic abilities and a talent for fashion design. Cardi identified with the lead character. While all of her friends wore the latest fashions, Cardi dressed in hot pink and purple like Raven.

> "My mom used to cry a lot because she used to be scared that I would fall asleep and die of an asthma attack."[8]
>
> —Cardi B

A Good Student Gone Bad

Cardi's hours in front of the television led her to develop a love for performing. This inspired her to attend Renaissance High School for Music Theater & Technology, which is affiliated with the Lincoln Center for the Performing Arts. Lincoln Center is home to a number of world-renowned performing arts organizations, including the New York Philharmonic, the Metropolitan Opera, Jazz at Lincoln Center, and the New York City Ballet. Students at Renaissance High attend performances at the Lincoln Center and at professional theater productions in New York's famed Broadway district.

Cardi says her mother pushed her to study hard and do her homework. Her teachers also encouraged her, telling her she was smart and had the potential to achieve her dreams. Cardi says she always raised her hand in class, was outspoken with her opinions, and participated in every class activity. Cardi also loved reading, and she says her favorite books were *To Kill a Mockingbird* by Harper Lee and *Their Eyes Were Watching God* by Zora Neale Hurston. Another favorite, *The Coldest Winter Ever*, is about the hip-hop–loving daughter of a drug kingpin in Brooklyn. It was written by rapper and political activist Sister Souljah. Cardi describes *The Coldest Winter Ever* as "a hood book, but it's really good. The main character is like my alter ego. She is a bad girl. I like a bit of bad-girl [stuff]."[9]

With her bad-girl attitude, Cardi was the class clown who often teased people for fun. But her outgoing personality made her a standout performer in the musical plays staged at Renaissance High. Despite her success at school, she felt torn between school and a need to rebel against her mother's restrictions. This led her to attend what she calls hooky parties—afternoon gatherings in friends' apartments when parents were not present.

The parties took precedence over school, and Cardi's grades slumped. She was expelled from Renaissance High when she was sixteen. She later said she chose her friends over her education. By that time, many of her friends were members of the notorious East Coast Bloods street gang, also known as the Brims. As Cardi later recalled, "My mom tried to stop me from all of that, but I still did it. I joined a gang. If she had let me out as often as I wanted to, I probably would be dead or got my face cut up."[10]

Cardi does not resent her mother's attempts to prevent her from going down the wrong path. Most of her high school friends ended up in jail or became teen mothers with limited options in life. Although Cardi resented her mother's tough love when she was growing up, today she credits it for her success. She has even remarked that she will follow her mom's example when raising her daughter: "I'm going to be very strict. Like, you can *have* whatever you want, but you can't *do* whatever you want."[11]

Becoming a Stripper

When Cardi was kicked out of high school, she did not tell her mother. While pretending to go to school, she spent her days hanging out with her friends. Her mother discovered the ruse and kicked Cardi out of the house. Cardi got a full-time job working the late-night shift at a small grocery store called the Amish Market, where she made $250 a week. She also took courses at the Borough of Manhattan Community College, located down the street from the market. Cardi studied history,

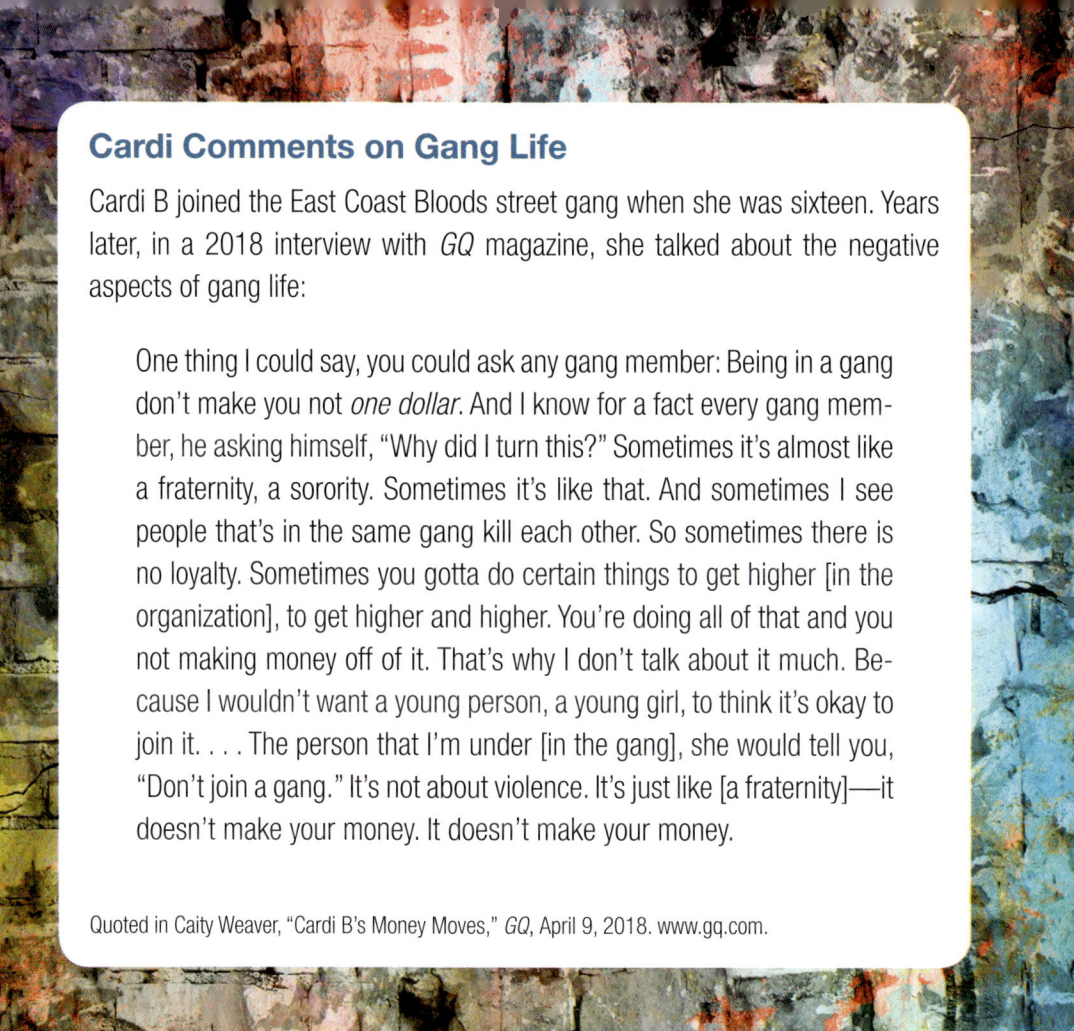

Cardi Comments on Gang Life

Cardi B joined the East Coast Bloods street gang when she was sixteen. Years later, in a 2018 interview with *GQ* magazine, she talked about the negative aspects of gang life:

> One thing I could say, you could ask any gang member: Being in a gang don't make you not *one dollar*. And I know for a fact every gang member, he asking himself, "Why did I turn this?" Sometimes it's almost like a fraternity, a sorority. Sometimes it's like that. And sometimes I see people that's in the same gang kill each other. So sometimes there is no loyalty. Sometimes you gotta do certain things to get higher [in the organization], to get higher and higher. You're doing all of that and you not making money off of it. That's why I don't talk about it much. Because I wouldn't want a young person, a young girl, to think it's okay to join it. . . . The person that I'm under [in the gang], she would tell you, "Don't join a gang." It's not about violence. It's just like [a fraternity]—it doesn't make your money. It doesn't make your money.

Quoted in Caity Weaver, "Cardi B's Money Moves," *GQ*, April 9, 2018. www.gq.com.

political science, and French. The struggle to balance work and school was too much, however, and she dropped out of college after a few semesters.

Cardi's life was complicated by her domestic situation. Her living arrangement was far from ideal. She and her boyfriend at the time were living with his mother. As Cardi recalls, "There was two pit bulls in that house, and I had asthma. There was bedbugs, too. On top of that, I felt like my . . . boyfriend was cheating on me, but it was like even if he was cheating on me, I still can't leave because—where was I gonna go?"[12] Cardi often complained to the market manager, saying she could not afford her own apartment with her low salary. The manager suggested she

Cardi took courses at the Borough of Manhattan Community College (pictured). She dropped out after a few semesters.

could earn much more money as a stripper at the New York Dolls Gentleman's Club, which was across the street from the Amish Market. Cardi decided to audition. On her way home from work at 4 a.m., she practiced acrobatic stripper pole dances on the hand poles of empty subway cars.

Cardi was eventually fired from the market for being late, having a bad attitude, and giving her coworkers large discounts on food and toiletries. In 2011, when she was almost nineteen years old, she walked across the street to the strip club. After an audition, she was hired to dance topless. However, as Cardi later recalled, she had reservations about her new job: "The first time I stripped I was really embarrassed. I felt like I could hear my parents in the back of my mind. . . . I felt so disgusted."[13]

Cardi felt guilty about her new line of work and says she would cry with shame whenever she imagined the faces of her parents watching her dance. She lied about her new job, telling her mother she was babysitting for a rich white couple. But she did not feel bad about the money she was making. On Cardi's first day as a stripper, she earned $300 in eight hours, more than her weekly salary at the Amish Market.

Cardi saved her money, got out of her toxic relationship, and moved into her own apartment. She also returned to school but dropped out again, this time because she was working six nights a week from 8 p.m. to 4 a.m.

Dangerous Enhancements

Cardi's stint at New York Dolls lasted about two months. While there, she built up enough confidence to look for work at clubs that catered to wealthier customers. However, Cardi, who is naturally thin, realized that surgical enhancements could help her make more money as a stripper.

Driven to achieve success, Cardi underwent surgery to augment her breasts and buttocks. But she could not afford an expensive Manhattan plastic surgeon. She had her breasts augmented in the Dominican Republic, where doctors charge much less for the procedure. The story of Cardi's 2014 butt enhancement has been discussed in numerous cautionary articles on the Internet. A butt enhancement procedure from a licensed US doctor can cost around $7,000. A patient might receive surgical implants or undergo other procedures approved by the Food and Drug Administration, the US government agency that regulates drugs and medical devices.

Cardi could not afford a legitimate procedure, so she visited a basement apartment in the Queens neighborhood of New York, where she paid a woman $800 for a butt enhancement. The woman—who was not a doctor—injected an unknown substance into Cardi's rear end, most likely a filler made from a synthetic substance called silicone oil or hydrogel. The injection, given with a very large needle, increased the size of Cardi's rear end, but the procedure was done without anesthetic. Cardi says, "It was the craziest pain ever. I felt like I was gonna pass out. I felt a little dizzy. And it leaks for, like, five days."[14]

Cardi B is lucky to be alive. The type of silicone injection she received can cause many serious complications, including inflammation, infection, bleeding, scarring, nerve damage, and—in some cases—death. Despite the pain, Cardi went back for a second injection. By that time, the woman was in jail; an injection had killed one of her clients. In 2018 Cardi was still worried about the injection, but since there is nothing she can do about it now, she is just hoping for the best.

Aiming Higher

Stripping helped Cardi achieve independence. On her best nights, she says, she made up to $3,000. But strip clubs are harsh environments. The women who work in them often suffer from emotional problems, drug addictions, and unstable relationships. The

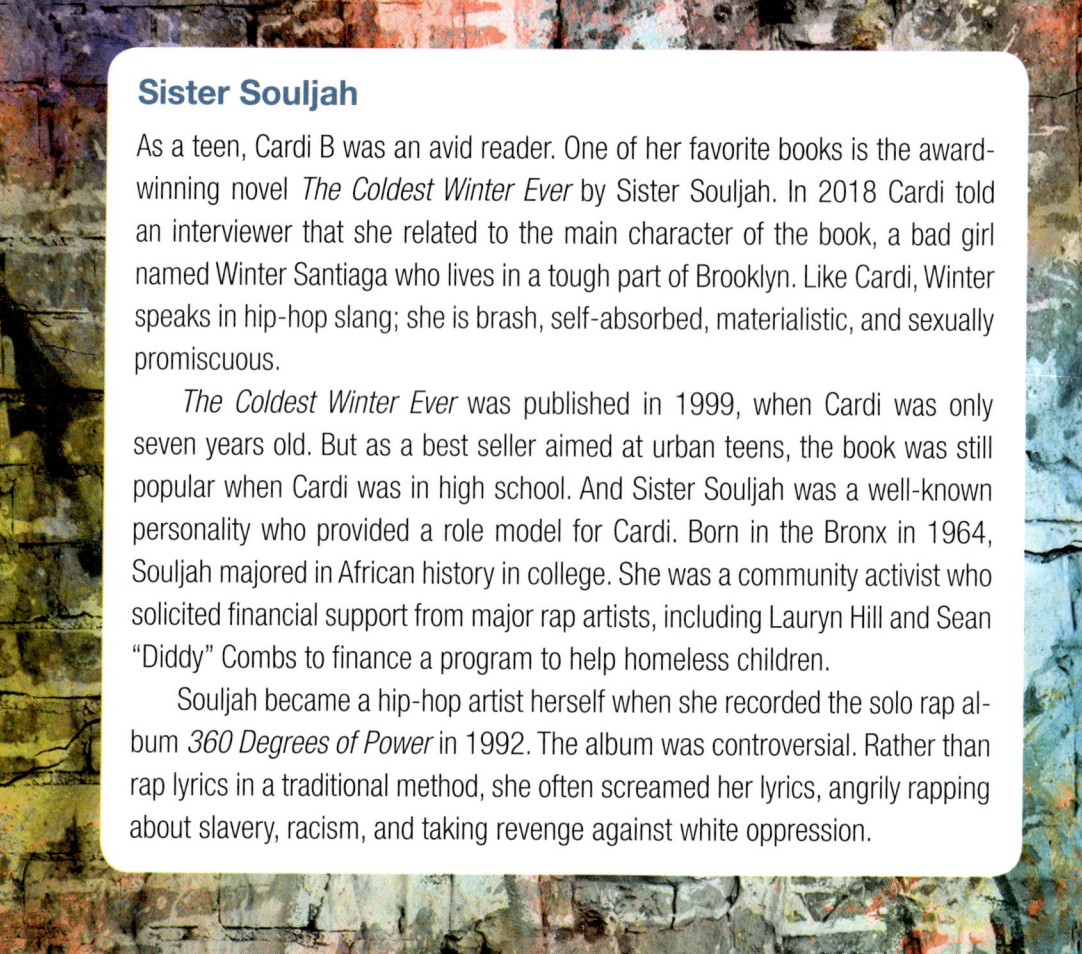

Sister Souljah

As a teen, Cardi B was an avid reader. One of her favorite books is the award-winning novel *The Coldest Winter Ever* by Sister Souljah. In 2018 Cardi told an interviewer that she related to the main character of the book, a bad girl named Winter Santiaga who lives in a tough part of Brooklyn. Like Cardi, Winter speaks in hip-hop slang; she is brash, self-absorbed, materialistic, and sexually promiscuous.

The Coldest Winter Ever was published in 1999, when Cardi was only seven years old. But as a best seller aimed at urban teens, the book was still popular when Cardi was in high school. And Sister Souljah was a well-known personality who provided a role model for Cardi. Born in the Bronx in 1964, Souljah majored in African history in college. She was a community activist who solicited financial support from major rap artists, including Lauryn Hill and Sean "Diddy" Combs to finance a program to help homeless children.

Souljah became a hip-hop artist herself when she recorded the solo rap album *360 Degrees of Power* in 1992. The album was controversial. Rather than rap lyrics in a traditional method, she often screamed her lyrics, angrily rapping about slavery, racism, and taking revenge against white oppression.

men who frequent them often degrade the dancers. "A lot of these men are gonna make you feel like you're trash,"[15] she says.

Cardi never planned to spend her life working in an industry that values sexuality over talent and intelligence. On her first day at New York Dolls, she vowed to quit stripping at age twenty-five; she wanted to settle down and have a baby. Cardi stripped for the last time on October 11, 2015, her twenty-third birthday. By that time, she had saved $35,000 and knew she could use her outsized personality, good looks, and intellect to achieve something more for herself. She also understood she could utilize the power of social media to take her career to another level.

BUILDING A FOLLOWING

Social media influencers are commonplace today. Online personalities routinely promote themselves and their brands on Instagram, Twitter, and Facebook. But in 2011, when Cardi B began posting her attention-grabbing selfies, memes, and videos, social media influencers were much less prominent. Cardi was ahead of her time. She understood that she could leverage her status as a popular New York stripper to build a social media following that would help her achieve fame. By 2013 her Instagram and Tumblr accounts had attracted many admirers, including local bartenders, bouncers, and club regulars—people she calls "little drug dealers and scammers."[16]

Cardi's videos attracted the most likes. While speaking directly into her phone's camera, she showed off her vivacious personality and enhanced curves while reeling off hilarious, obscenity-laden observations at a hundred miles an hour. She gabbed about whatever came into her head at the moment. Although most people tend to be careful about what they say online, Cardi discussed her family, poverty, sex life, and work as a stripper with unfiltered honesty. As journalist Angie Liu writes, "In her Instagram videos, Cardi is often seen without her hair done, without makeup, and sometimes, even without clothes."[17]

Building the Cardi Brand

Many people found Cardi's honesty refreshing and entertaining, and they began sharing her posts. By 2014 some of Cardi's videos were attracting hundreds of thousands of comments and likes. She expanded her fan base by creating videos that fell into three general categories: those addressed to women, those aimed at men, and trash-talk clips targeting detractors. Cardi told women how to use their feminine powers to manipulate men. As an unnamed staff member at the website Jezebel put it, "There was a Cardi B Instagram vid that changed my life where she talked about how she was in school but then started stripping and then the Russian strippers taught her how to con men for money."[18] In videos where Cardi speaks to men, she warns them not to underestimate her or other women. One clip in particular helped push Cardi into the social media stratosphere. The thirteen-second video reveals her honesty, her humor, and her way with words: "People be asking me, 'What do you does? Are you a model? Are you a comedian or something?' Nah, I ain't none of that.... I'm a stripper.... I'm about the shmoney."[19]

Although Cardi could make fun of herself, she would not put up with similar comments from people who spewed ugly remarks about her looks, her accent, or her work as a stripper. She has been known to post scathing, vulgar tirades that are wickedly funny or, sometimes, frightening. She has even responded to other people's nastiness by posting a clip that simply showed her laughing insanely for fifteen seconds.

A Microcelebrity

Cardi claims her viral social media success was unintentional because she was just being herself. But her impromptu videos began attracting throngs of young women who were eager to hear her comments and advice on subjects that were important to them. Cardi's Instagram account grew to around 1 million followers by the end of 2014. She used her online popularity to organize live events where fans paid admission to hang out with her in nightclubs.

Cardi's social media presence made her a microcelebrity—that is, someone who is famous among a group of followers who share similar interests. This attracted the attention of promoters and advertisers who paid Cardi to wear their fashions or mention their products in her posts. The budget-friendly online retailer

Fashion Nova was the first to recognize the power of Cardi's microcelebrity. As Cardi B's stylist Kollin Carter explains, "Fashion Nova will always be super close to [Cardi]. That was a brand that was [working with] her before anybody believed in her. . . . Fashion Nova always has a perfect denim for her. They cater to women with curves."[20] Cardi continued to work with the brand after achieving superstar status; she launched the Cardi B x Fashion Nova clothing line in 2018. The collection included around ninety pieces, including denim dresses, pants, and outerwear.

Cardi teamed up with clothing retailer Fashion Nova to come up with her own fashion line. She appeared at the launch of the line, Cardi B x Fashion Nova, in Los Angeles in 2018.

Cardi was attractive to online retailers like Fashion Nova because of her unapologetic honesty. If she did not like something, she would let it be known, often in the most basic terms. But if Cardi wore a certain brand of jeans, followers could assume she really liked them. As Liu explains, "[Cardi is] a talented, authentic self-starter who bends the rules to suit her needs. She's on a different wavelength that fans and brands alike want to latch on to."[21]

Cardi's honesty served another positive purpose for her brand. By discussing her body enhancements, promiscuity, and other issues, she was immune to scandal. No one could ever reveal embarrassing secrets about Cardi after she herself had discussed them with her millions of followers.

> "[Cardi is] a talented, authentic self-starter who bends the rules to suit her needs. She's on a different wavelength that fans and brands alike want to latch on to."[21]
>
> —Angie Liu, journalist

Stealing the Show

Cardi's microcelebrity attracted followers who had powerful jobs in the entertainment industry. In 2015—only a month after she stopped stripping—producers of a long-running VH1 reality television show cast her to appear in season six of *Love & Hip-Hop: New York*. As the show's press release stated, "Firecracker and Instagram sensation Cardi B leaps from the pages of [Instagram] to the small screen with a bang!"[22]

When Cardi appeared on *Love & Hip-Hop,* the series was focused on women who struggled personally and professionally in the male-dominated hip-hop industry. The show, which can be as dramatic as any soap opera, features Grammy winners, DJs, managers, and music producers. *Love & Hip-Hop* also had a revolving cast of struggling rappers, glamour models, dancers, and others who strive on the margins of the industry. The show exposes the love lives, family relationships, lofty ambitions, and shattered dreams of cast members.

The stars of season six of *Love & Hip-Hop* were supposed to be rapper Remy Ma and her husband, Papoose. Ma had just been released from prison after serving six years on assault and illegal weapons charges. Producers expected Ma's hardened personality to draw in viewers. Cardi was cast in a minor role as a struggling stripper. However, it was apparent by the show's fourth episode that Ma's star power could not compete with Cardi's spontaneous outbursts, whip-smart wit, and revealing outfits.

Cardi came to dominate what is called the reaction room, a staple of reality shows where cast members look directly into the camera to express their anger, frustration, and innermost thoughts. The reaction room is where viewers come to love—or hate—reality show cast members, and it is where stars are born. As journalist Clover Hope explains, "Besides being loud, strange, funny and self-aware—all the right reality ingredients—she's debatably real in a world that's blatantly fabricated, which makes her a welcome face to fans thirsting for honest characters."[23]

With her years of practice making viral videos, Cardi's quotable comments made her the breakout cast member of *Love & Hip-Hop*. In her unique style, Cardi explained that the producers bet on the wrong woman when they chose to feature Remy Ma: "Yo, it's so crazy, like, them [producers] really doubted me. It's like, why would y'all doubt me? Like, I have seven hundred thousand bajillion followers. I'm telling them like, 'Yo, I have a brand. I'm not even an artist and I fill out clubs.'. . . But they didn't care about that. They just wanted to make me look as a stripper."[24]

Although Cardi wanted to move beyond her stripper past, many of the new Instagram followers she acquired from *Love & Hip-Hop* would not let her. Cardi notes that as her fame increased, the comments on her Instagram feed grew increasingly

> "Yo, it's so crazy, like, them [producers] really doubted me. It's like, why would y'all doubt me? Like, I have seven hundred thousand bajillion followers. I'm telling them like, 'Yo, I have a brand.'"[24]
>
> —Cardi B

Rapper Remy Ma performs at the Hot 97 Summer Jam in 2018. Ma starred in season six of *Love & Hip-Hop* along with Cardi.

nasty. She says she would even cry sometimes when people made fun of her looks, called her dumb, mocked her accent, or scolded her for stripping. Cardi answered her critics: "A lot of people think I'm just a dumb ass . . . because I can't talk English properly and it's just like, yo if I was dumb, I would not be in the position that I'm in. It's just like damn everybody wants to be famous but, like, people don't realize being famous don't make you like rich. Like, yo you really gotta work to get rich."[25]

Hip-Hop Debut

As Cardi noted in her own way, cast members on reality shows like *Love & Hip-Hop* do not get paid very much. But Cardi had other plans. She began her hip-hop career in November 2015, around the same time she was stealing the show on *Love & Hip-Hop*. Her rap debut was initially inspired by her manager, a man named Shaft who handled her social media career. Shaft noticed that when Cardi listened to rap music she would make up her own lyrics, stringing together verses filled with comical lines. Shaft

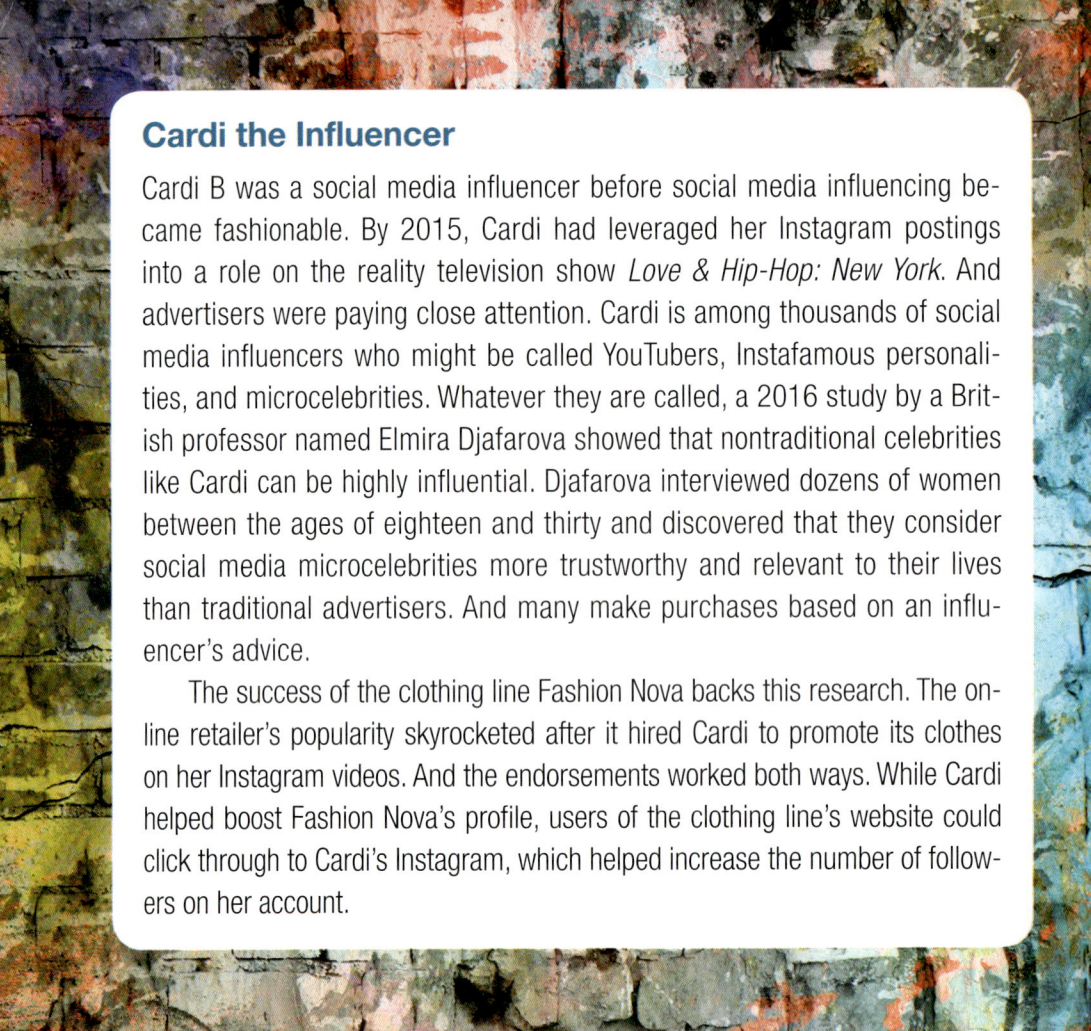

Cardi the Influencer

Cardi B was a social media influencer before social media influencing became fashionable. By 2015, Cardi had leveraged her Instagram postings into a role on the reality television show *Love & Hip-Hop: New York*. And advertisers were paying close attention. Cardi is among thousands of social media influencers who might be called YouTubers, Instafamous personalities, and microcelebrities. Whatever they are called, a 2016 study by a British professor named Elmira Djafarova showed that nontraditional celebrities like Cardi can be highly influential. Djafarova interviewed dozens of women between the ages of eighteen and thirty and discovered that they consider social media microcelebrities more trustworthy and relevant to their lives than traditional advertisers. And many make purchases based on an influencer's advice.

The success of the clothing line Fashion Nova backs this research. The online retailer's popularity skyrocketed after it hired Cardi to promote its clothes on her Instagram videos. And the endorsements worked both ways. While Cardi helped boost Fashion Nova's profile, users of the clothing line's website could click through to Cardi's Instagram, which helped increase the number of followers on her account.

asked her if she ever considered rapping. Cardi laughed at the suggestion. But after thinking it over, she realized that she could make some money writing a song, posting a video on YouTube, and publicizing it on her Instagram account. She might even be able to market the song on Apple Music.

Cardi went into the recording studio and freestyled (improvised verses) to some prerecorded beats. She discovered she did not have a good flow, or smooth, distinctive delivery. But Cardi set her mind on becoming a good rapper and practiced continually until she developed a unique flow. And unlike many rappers who have a team of writers creating their verses, Cardi began writing her own bars.

Cardi made her hip-hop debut singing with Jamaican singer Shaggy on a remix of the song "Boom Boom." She only had one verse, and her flow was not fully developed. But the line was memorable as she referred to herself as Cardi Bartier, a mashup of Bacardi rum and Cartier jewelry. Although it was Cardi's first musical outing, Shaggy said he was glad to work with her: "I was already a fan of hers and her big personality on *Love and Hip Hop*. I found her to be the highlight of the show. I'm happy that she's the breakout star of the show. It was a pleasure to have worked with her."[26] Cardi made her music video debut in "Cheap Ass Weave," a song she wrote about bad hair extensions based on "Queen's Speech 4," a song by English rapper Lady Leshurr.

Cardi made her hip-hop debut with Jamaican singer Shaggy (pictured) on a remix of the song "Boom Boom" in 2015.

Breaking the Internet

By March 2016, Cardi was breaking the Internet with every new episode of *Love & Hip-Hop*. And the show even gave her material for her hip-hop songs. In one of the most memorable scenes from *Love & Hip-Hop*, Cardi is romantically interested in a rapper called DJ Self. However, when he brings another woman to a party, Cardi becomes very jealous. She screams at Self: "A girl have beef with me, she gonna have beef with me." Cardi then drops her voice into a scary babyish growl and utters the word "foreva."[27] Fans loved the scene, which went viral with multiple memes and gifs. This prompted Cardi to write the track "Foreva," which was featured on her first mixtape, *Gangsta Bitch Music, Vol. 1*.

"Foreva" was a late addition to that mixtape, which Cardi had been working on for about a year. Although some rappers make a mixtape in a few months, Cardi says she took the project very seriously: "Everything I do, it takes a lot of time for me to do it because only the best sells, you know? If you want people to take you seriously, you gotta do the best. . . . Only great things sell."[28]

What Cardi was selling on her first mixtape was the same thing she had been marketing for several years—herself. As with her Instagram videos, Cardi's tracks on *Gangsta Bitch Music, Vol. 1* take aim at lying men and people who make nasty comments about her while she brags about herself. On "Sauce Boyz," she roasts guys who make grand claims that they cannot back up with cash. On "Everything," Cardi talks about the money she earned as a successful stripper. And as music journalist Craig Jenkins notes, "There's a laugh-out-loud quotable [statement per] minute, partly because Cardi hasn't all the way figured out this rap thing but also because she is deadly at roasting on the fly. . . . There's heart and smarts fueling the Cardi B

> "Everything I do, it takes a lot of time for me to do it because only the best sells, you know? If you want people to take you seriously, you gotta do the best."[28]
>
> —Cardi B

Bringing the Music to *Love & Hip-Hop*

Before Cardi B became the breakout star on the reality show *Love & Hip-Hop: New York*, it was a standard joke that no one on the show cared about hip-hop music. Most cast members were either washed-up rappers with one hit song or producers whose glory days were long past. But as music journalist Craig Jenkins notes, with the release of her first mixtape, *Gangsta Bitch Music, Vol. 1*, Cardi B helped bring hip-hop music back to *Love & Hip-Hop*:

> The typical *Love and Hip-Hop* season is an endless array of launch parties for songs you never hear again after the credits roll, most of them bad and forgettable. Personal vendettas rise and fall over middling beats and questionable guest verses. . . . Cardi is a reminder of the magical, absurd unpredictability of regular . . . people that birthed reality TV in the first place. Her new mixtape *Gangsta Bitch Music Vol. 1* is easily the most enjoyable body of music to come out of *Love and Hip-Hop*. . . . What makes [the mixtape] work is that the persona on the show is her persona on the record is her persona on Instagram and Twitter. . . . With Cardi, what you see is what you get, and what you get is stone cold realness.

> Craig Jenkins, "Cardi B's 'Gangsta Bitch Music Vol. 1' Is the First Good Record to Come Out of 'Love and Hip-Hop,'" Vice, March 9, 2016. www.vice.com.

spectacle, and *Gangsta Bitch Music*, however clumsily at times, succeeds in delivering the full picture."[29]

With her laughable quotes and deadly roasts, Cardi does not need complex musical tracks to back her bars. She mostly relies on sparse musical samples backed by trap beats. Trap rap can be identified by its distinctive double- or triple-time beats. Drummers play the hyper beats on a hi-hat—a pair of cymbals that can be opened and closed with a foot pedal.

Released at the height of Cardi's skyrocketing reality television fame, *Gangsta Bitch Music, Vol. 1* reached number twenty on the

Billboard Top Rap Albums chart and number twenty-seven on the Independent Albums chart. Cardi promoted the mixtape on the cable television talk show circuit, appearing on *Uncommon Sense with Charlemagne* and *Kocktails with Khloé*.

Gangsta Laughs

After two seasons, Cardi decided to quit *Love & Hip-Hop: New York* in 2017. By this time, her career was booming. She signed an endorsement deal with the Romantic Depot, a chain of lingerie stores. She also partnered with MAC Cosmetics and fashion designer Rio Uribe for a series of guest appearances at New York Fashion Week. Additionally, Cardi found time to record another mixtape, *Gangsta Bitch Music, Vol. 2*.

Cardi is in fine form on her second mixtape, spitting raw, raunchy, and audacious rhymes. And, as usual, her bars can be side-splittingly funny. As Cardi explains, "Music is my passion, so I see myself as a rapper. I also love making people laugh—there's a part of my brain that likes to make jokes every two seconds. I feel like there are little people working in there! So, I'm a comedian as well as a rapper—a comedian-rapper."[30]

The comedian in Cardi, combined with her unabashed honesty, might be the key to her success. As Liu explains, "I don't know if Cardi ever meant for her personality to become her 'brand' but the fact that she hasn't had to change her outspokenness in the face of fame is admirable. . . . How can someone be vulgar but so sweet and charming at the same time? It's really an art, and one that she has perfected."[31]

While some rappers take themselves very seriously, Cardi understands that her honesty and humor can be an antidote to the anxiety many people feel in their daily lives. Cardi transitioned from a microcelebrity to a respectable rapper while inspiring fans across the spectrum to love her art in all its vulgar glory.

THE HOTTEST THING IN HIP-HOP

Cardi B's career can be viewed as a series of giant—if unlikely—leaps forward. Very few strippers become top-trending Instagram celebrities. And fewer social media microcelebrities make entertainment headlines starring in reality shows like *Love & Hip-Hop: New York*. But Cardi's biggest step up was associated with her rap career. In 2017, after releasing her second mixtape, *Gangsta Bitch Music, Vol. 2*, Cardi landed a multimillion-dollar record contract with Atlantic Records. At that time, Cardi had only been rapping for two years. By way of comparison, one of Cardi's main hip-hop competitors, Nicki Minaj, had been rapping and recording for more than eight years before signing with a major label. And as the superstar rapper Drake says in the song "Two Birds, One Stone," 98 percent of people trying to make it as rappers fail. The reality is probably closer to 99.9 percent.

Cardi was a relative latecomer to the hip-hop game, but as every rapper knows, originality is the key to success. And Cardi was able to succeed because she is one of a kind. With a few well-chosen syllables, she can tell a story that gets listeners twerking and popping, as she would say.

Cardi had never rapped in front of an audience when she was signed as an opening act for the East Coast hip-hop group the Lox. Formed in Yonkers, New York, in 1994, the Lox achieved national prominence in 1997, when members collaborated with Sean "Diddy" Combs on the hit single "It's All About the Benjamins." However, the group struggled for many years before releasing *Filthy America . . . It's Beautiful* (2016), its first album in sixteen years. During the group's new album tour, Cardi performed at their Reading, Pennsylvania, concert. This might seem like an improbable pairing; after all, Cardi was only five years old when "It's All About the Benjamins" was released. But the February 2017 concert, which also featured established rappers Remy Ma and Lil' Kim, helped introduce Cardi's music to an older generation of hip-hop fans.

Setting Off with Offset

Cardi's rising profile caught the eye of more than a few OGs (original gangstas) who saw her on the Lox tour. The rapper Offset also found himself very interested in Cardi after hearing her mixtapes and seeing her on television. Offset found success as a member of the hip-hop trio Migos, which he founded in Atlanta with his cousins Takeoff and Quavo. Migos is known for its top-ten hip-hop party songs and rap anthems, such as "Bad and Boujee" (2016) and "Stir Fry" (2017).

Offset had his publicist call Cardi and set up a date. The couple attended a Super Bowl party and soon began dating. Offset was instantly smitten with Cardi: "She is real solid. . . . She's herself, man. I seen her develop from the trenches all the way up, and I like how she did it. I respect her grind as a woman. She came to the game with some gangsta [stuff]. I like that."[32]

Offset soon had Cardi's name tattooed on his neck. On Valentine's Day 2017, Cardi posted a video of her and Offset on Instagram, confirming relationship rumors that had been swirling among fans for a month. But Cardi and Offset ran hot and cold. In March, Cardi refused to admit she was dating someone she referred to only as a guy from Atlanta. Then, in May, the two were seen together at the prestigious Met Gala, an annual benefit of the Metropolitan Museum of Art's Costume Institute in New York City. Cardi remained noncom-

> "She is real solid. . . . She's herself, man. I seen her develop from the trenches all the way up, and I like how she did it."[32]
>
> —Rapper Offset

Cardi B performs with rapper Offset at the Jimmy Kimmel Live! show in 2019. The two were married in 2017 and had a daughter in 2018.

mittal when asked about Offset, discussing him in context with his band in an interview with *Fader* magazine: "It's been a blessing, me meeting him and meeting his friends [in Migos]. I see how hard they work. And that motivated me to work even harder. And I see how good things are going for them and how popping it is to be number one. And I'm like, I want that."[33]

In July an Instagram post showed Cardi and Offset backstage at a Meek Mill concert. Cardi was wearing a chain and dazzling diamond pendant that Offset had presented to her. It was later revealed to be a $60,000 custom-made piece of jewelry created by celebrity jeweler Elliot Avianne. The pendant, blanketed in thirty-five karats of diamonds, is modeled on Cardi's hand, complete with blood-red fingernails. A tiny red bandana, a symbol of the Bloods street gang, was wrapped around the wrist part of the pendant.

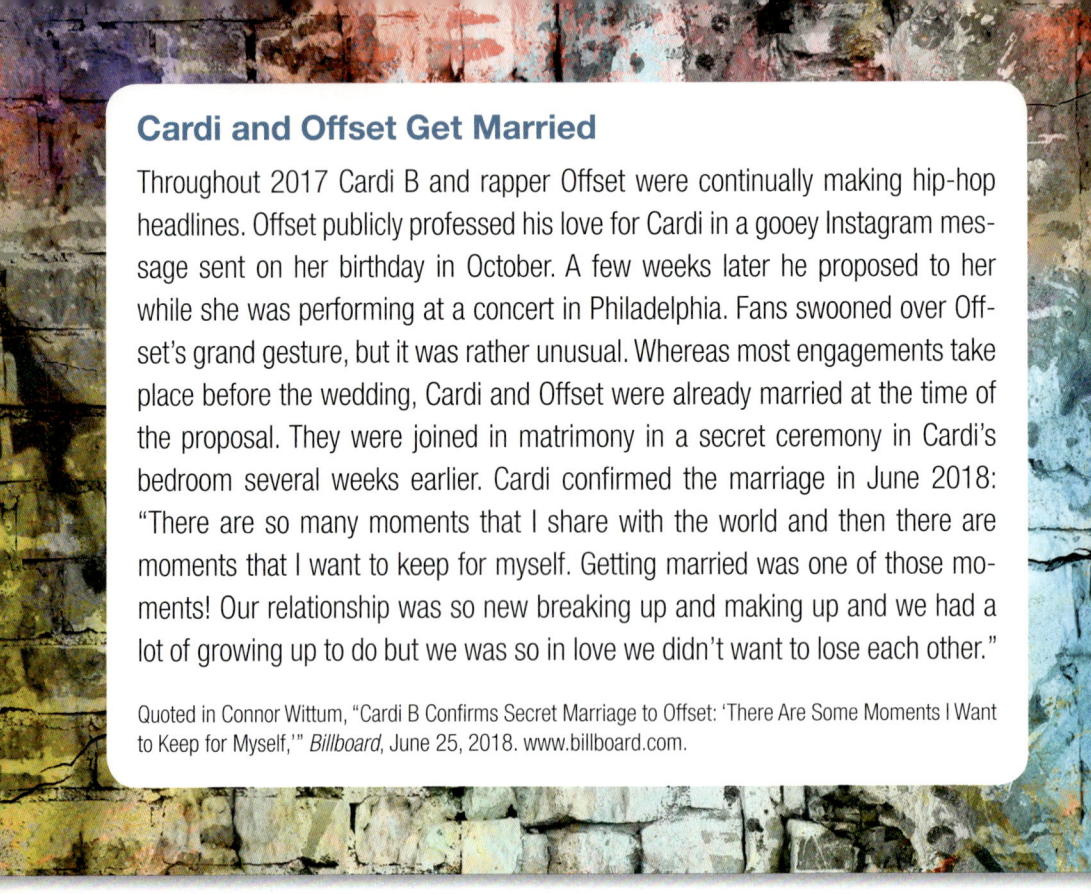

Cardi and Offset Get Married

Throughout 2017 Cardi B and rapper Offset were continually making hip-hop headlines. Offset publicly professed his love for Cardi in a gooey Instagram message sent on her birthday in October. A few weeks later he proposed to her while she was performing at a concert in Philadelphia. Fans swooned over Offset's grand gesture, but it was rather unusual. Whereas most engagements take place before the wedding, Cardi and Offset were already married at the time of the proposal. They were joined in matrimony in a secret ceremony in Cardi's bedroom several weeks earlier. Cardi confirmed the marriage in June 2018: "There are so many moments that I share with the world and then there are moments that I want to keep for myself. Getting married was one of those moments! Our relationship was so new breaking up and making up and we had a lot of growing up to do but we was so in love we didn't want to lose each other."

Quoted in Connor Wittum, "Cardi B Confirms Secret Marriage to Offset: 'There Are Some Moments I Want to Keep for Myself,'" *Billboard*, June 25, 2018. www.billboard.com.

The gang reference created controversy when Avianne tweeted "Bloody Moves"[34] with a photo of the gift. Although Cardi continued to deny it, some believed she was still a member of the Bloods.

Offset continued to woo Cardi in a very public manner. When Cardi celebrated her twenty-fifth birthday in October 2017, Offset was on tour with Migos in New Zealand. But he was not too preoccupied to send a birthday greeting on Instagram: "HAPPY B DAY U ARE AMAZING TO ME YOU GOT IT OUT DA MUDD NO HELP NOBODY WAS BELIEVING AT FIRST BUT THAT MADE YOU GO HARDER U NOT WEAK U TAKE CARE YA WHOLE FAMILY AND ME I LOVE YOU."[35] The message was sent with an intimate video of Cardi and Offset kissing. About a week later, Cardi posted an Instagram selfie with a one-word caption: "single."[36] The next day, as breakup rumors were trending on social media, Cardi did an about-face and posted she was still head over heels in love with Offset, who she considered a gift to her from God.

Cardi's Clout

Cardi's reluctance to commit to Offset might be traced to his background. When Offset met Cardi, he had three children with three different women and also had a lengthy arrest record. Additionally, Cardi was extremely busy. In April 2017 she appeared in a video that was part of the long-running A-Z of Music series by the youth-centric fashion and culture magazine *i-D*. The video features a style of music or musical idea for each letter of the alphabet, starting with *Afropunk* and ending with *zing* (a slang term for a clever comment). Each concept is accompanied by a short performance from a musician or fashion icon. Cardi joked around (as usual) with a boastful chant and a little dance for her V for *viral* segment.

Cardi was also working in television, appearing on the VH1 game show *Hip-Hop Squares*. The show was modeled after the classic game show *Hollywood Squares*, which ran on NBC from 1966 to 1981. The updated version featured two rappers competing with one another to correctly answer questions posed by the host, rapper Ice Cube. Correct answers win $1,000 to $2,000, with the money going to members of the studio audience. Cardi starred on the celebrity panel for two episodes in March and April.

In May, Cardi won her first award nominations as a rap artist. The BET Hip Hop Awards nominated Cardi for the Best New Artist and Best Female Hip Hop Artist awards. When she learned of the nominations, her reaction was pure Cardi. She had just come out of the shower and was wearing nothing but a large yellow towel and shower cap. That did not stop Cardi from broadcasting her reaction live on Instagram as she jumped up and down, laughing loudly with tears of joy running down her face. The video, which quickly generated over 172,000 likes and 5,400 comments, was shared by fans on Twitter, prompting Cardi's response: "B***h is trending."[37]

After she calmed down, Cardi was unusually humble. She tweeted a heartfelt thanks to BET and gave a shout-out to up-and-coming female rappers Katie Got Bandz, Cupcakke, and Kash Doll. When the awards show aired in June 2017, Cardi lost the Best New Artist award to Chance the Rapper, and Remy Ma claimed the award for Best Female Hip Hop Artist. Cardi and Offset attended the BET Hip Hop Awards separately, but most of the attention was focused on Cardi's high-energy performance at the after-party.

Some people felt that Cardi was robbed of a win in the female hip-hop artist category. As hip-hop journalist Aaron Williams noted, none of the other nominees—Nicki Minaj, Missy Elliott, and Remy Ma—had dropped an album or mixtape in the previous year: "Which leaves Cardi B as one of the only women who released a full project recently. While she did get to rock the after-party stage, and did a damn fine job as well, she deserved much more. Out of the nominees listed, she deserved that award the most."[38]

Cardi Makes Her Money Moves

Cardi did not feel robbed when Remy Ma won Best Female Hip Hop Artist. As one of Cardi's unnamed friends told the website Hollywood Life, "She wants Remy to win. She looks up to her, she's one of her idols. If she ends up getting it instead of Remy, it will feel weird."[39] Whatever Cardi's feelings, by the time the awards show was held, she was the hottest thing in hip-hop. Cardi's first single, "Bodak Yellow (Money Moves)"—often just called "Bodak Yellow"—had dropped about a week earlier and was rocketing up the charts.

"Bodak Yellow" is an homage to Florida rapper Kodak Black, whose 2015 song "No Flockin" inspired Cardi's flow on her debut single. But "No Flockin" was an unusual choice for Cardi. Most rappers trying to break into the game model their early tracks on number-one hits. For example, when Minaj released her debut mixtape, *Playtime Is Over*, in 2007, she used samples from some of the biggest hip-hop artists of the day, including Jay-Z, Lil Wayne, and DJ Khaled. "No Flockin" was hardly in the same league. The song was originally released in 2014 on Kodak Black's YouTube account and eventually peaked at number ninety-five on the *Billboard* Hot 100 singles chart when it was released on iTunes a year later. And the sparse, hypnotic trap rap

Cardi's first single, "Bodak Yellow," is an homage to Florida rapper Kodak Black (pictured). Black's 2015 song "No Flockin" inspired Cardi on her debut single.

arrangement behind "Bodak Yellow" is not usually considered a money-making sound. As music journalist Brittany Spanos explains, "'Bodak Yellow' is an unlikely Number One: a tough trap song with zero concessions to the mainstream, or even anything like a conventional pop hook."[40]

Whatever "Bodak Yellow" might seem to lack in commercial appeal is erased by the Cardi factor. From the first line, Cardi's bars are tough, defiant, and perfectly express her larger-than-life backstory. She lets listeners know that she does not have to dance anymore because she makes money moves that make her the boss. Cardi raps that her unnamed female rivals are in the club just to party, but

Kodak Black

Cardi B's breakout single "Bodak Yellow (Money Moves)" was inspired by rapper Kodak Black, who was born in 1997. Black's parents were Haitian immigrants, and he grew up in a public housing project in Pompano Beach, Florida. Black was seen as a hip-hop prodigy. He began rapping in the trap rap style when he was in elementary school, and he could often be found reading dictionaries and thesauruses to find interesting new words for his verses. He began performing under the stage name J-Black when he was twelve and released his first mixtape at age fifteen. Black was only seventeen when he recorded "No Flockin," the song Cardi B sampled for "Bodak Yellow." When Black released his debut studio album, *Painting Pictures* (2017), it reached number three on the *Billboard* 200 album chart.

Although Black has hit the charts with several records, his musical career has often been sidelined by his legal problems. He was arrested for a number of crimes between 2015 and 2017, including robbery, battery, rape, sexual assault, drug and firearms possession, and false imprisonment of a child. Black spent those years between recording studios, courtrooms, and prisons. While he remained free on bail in 2019, he was facing up to ten years in prison.

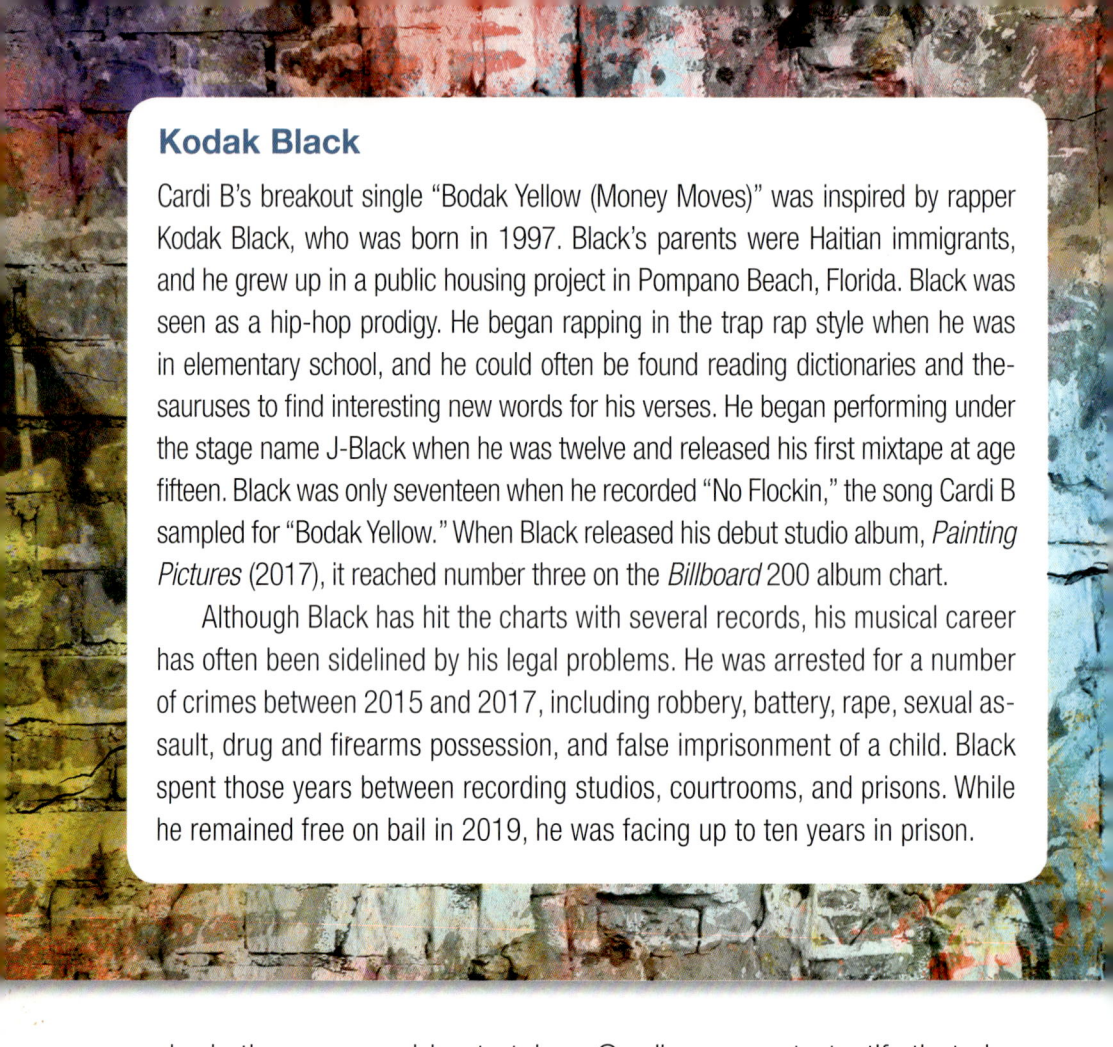

she is there as a paid entertainer. Cardi goes on to testify that she dropped two mixtapes in six months and works too hard to chill. And in case her online trolls were wondering, she earns enough to pay her mother's bills, wear designer fashions, and live in a great big house. Cardi describes what motivated her to write the aggressive lyrics to "Bodak Yellow": "[Haters expected] me to drop something trash. It just made me, like, 'Aha, I gotta study these other rappers. Study how to do something different from them. You know all these female rappers, they talking about they money, they talking about they cars, so it's like, what's something that I enjoy? I enjoy fights!"[41]

A Number-One Single

Cardi knew her fans would love her queen-of-the-hill proclamations. "Bodak Yellow" hit number one on the Hot 100 and stayed there for three weeks. Cardi was the fifth female rapper to lead the chart and only the second to do so as a solo act. It had been nearly twenty years since Lauryn Hill became the first female rapper to hit number one on the Hot 100 with the 1998 release "Doo Wop (That Thing)." And Cardi achieved something else that many rappers can only dream of: her debut single knocked superstar pop diva Taylor Swift's song "Look What You Made Me Do" out of the number-one spot. Cardi emphasized her achievement in 2018: "I built the fan base. No record label, no money, nothing can make you. You make yourself."[42]

> "I built the fan base. No record label, no money, nothing can make you. You make yourself."[42]
>
> —Cardi B

Every hit song has a good video to help pump up sales, and "Bodak Yellow" was no exception. The video was shot in the desert city of Dubai, located on the Persian Gulf, and features Cardi alternately dancing, riding a camel, and rapping while a full-grown cheetah watches impassively. The video racked up more than 809 million YouTube views. As music critic Tom Breihan writes, it is

> basically everything a rap video should be. It's Cardi, squeezed into a shiny black vinyl dress and holding a cheetah on a chain, leaning back on stone-temple stairs while telling you all the reasons you ain't [nothing]. . . . Her voice is a full-bodied New Yawk nasal bleat . . . [and] Cardi uses that voice to fill up . . . all the track's open space to project personality everywhere. It's a big, loud, brash, noisy song, and it's perfect.[43]

Reviewers in the music press loved "Bodak Yellow." *Pitchfork* magazine called it the best rap song of the year, and *Rolling Stone* included the song on its current list of the one hundred greatest songs of the century. *Rolling Stone* also proclaimed 2017 as Cardi B's year.

Cardi's debut single knocked Taylor Swift's (pictured) song "Look What You Made Me Do" out of the number-one spot on the Hot 100 chart.

Guest Appearances

As Cardi's star continued to rise, other rappers begged her to appear on their records. In September, Cardi and A$AP Rocky were featured on the single "No Limit" by rapper G-Eazy. Although Cardi only did one verse, some reviewers thought she stole the show as she rapped about her career taking off while the competition was running in place. G-Eazy said he did not mind Cardi getting most of the attention: "We sent the track to Cardi B and she killed it. I've been following her ever since she first started to buzz. I always wanted to connect with her. I met her at a show we played almost a year ago. I could tell right then and there she was going to be a super star."[44] Cardi's buzz helped draw attention to "No Limit," which hit number four on the Hot 100, making it G-Eazy's highest-charting song.

In October, Cardi made another buzzworthy guest appearance, this time with Offset's band, Migos. Cardi rapped on "MotorSport" alongside Nicki Minaj. Once again, Cardi drew more attention than the song's creators. Her verse won the Best Featured Verse award at the 2018 BET Hip Hop Awards. "MotorSport," which was the lead single from Migos's third studio album, *Culture II*, reached number six on the Hot 100. This gave Cardi another distinction: no female rapper had ever placed her first three singles in the top ten of the Hot 100 chart.

> "I've been following her ever since she first started to buzz. I always wanted to connect with her. I met her at a show we played almost a year ago. I could tell right then and there she was going to be a super star."[44]
>
> —Rapper G-Eazy

A Diamond in the Rough

Cardi's career plunged ahead at full speed. She wrapped up a successful 2017 by releasing her second single, "Bartier Cardi." Cardi is defiant and aggressive on the song as she tells listeners her body is covered in Cartier diamonds. The track's momentum builds steadily over a chilling trap rap sound as Cardi once again dispatches her critics in triple-time rhyme. As reviewer Sheldon Pearce writes, "Her phrases sway naturally, the same way her chatter does. She never minces words, and in these verses, her taunts and insults are even more cutting . . . her accent thrusting every word forward. She's more forceful and unambiguous as the song goes on, her tone dismissive. Even her ad-libs are kinetic."[45]

As 2017 drew to a close, there was little doubt that Cardi B was the year's dominant force in hip-hop. She began the year with the release of a mixtape that barely made a blip in the music press. She ended the year as one of the hottest record-breaking rappers anywhere. Cardi's face was featured on the cover of national magazines, and her comical quotes were burning up the Internet. While she attracted her share of negative attention, Bartier Cardi proved to the world she was a big, loud, brash diamond in the rough.

CHAPTER FOUR

HIP-HOP'S REIGNING QUEEN

Cardi B often refers to herself as a "regular, degular, shmegular girl from the Bronx,"[46] but there is nothing regular about her explosive ride to the top of the charts. After two out-of-nowhere smash hit singles in 2017, Cardi ascended the throne as the new reigning queen of hip-hop. She was instantly accepted in the worlds of fashion, entertainment, and popular culture, and her high-profile love affair and rap feuds kept her name in hip-hop headlines.

By early 2018, fans of Cardi's frenetic, over-the-top freestyle bars were begging for more. And they were not disappointed when Cardi dropped her long-awaited debut album, *Invasion of Privacy*, in April. As reviewer Rob Sheffield writes, "*Invasion of Privacy* is even better than everybody was hoping it would be, a whirlwind tour of Planet Cardi, a place where female warriors reign supreme. . . . [The album] is lavishly emotional, intimately personal, wildly funny."[47]

Crushing All Doubts

The head-spinning lyrics on *Invasion of Privacy* spread the news emanating from "Planet Cardi." Her bars cover her past, her newfound fame, and, of course, detailed accounts of her sex life. Cardi threatens nameless competitors and boasts about her wealth. And the high-profile guests featured on *Invasion of Privacy* prove that big-name rappers and singers want to get close to Cardi. Migos cowrote and performed on "Drip," an aggressive, synthesizer-heavy trap track filled with boasts and intimidating threats aimed at critics. Two of the biggest Latin rap stars, Puerto Rico's Bad Bunny and Colombia's J Balvin, helped Cardi celebrate her

Latina roots with Spanish-language breaks on the track "I Like It." The Latin trap sound on the track fuses elements of Southern trap rap, American R&B (rhythm and blues), pop, and Puerto Rican reggaeton.

> "[I'm just a] regular, degular, shmegular girl from the Bronx."[46]
> —Cardi B

Chance the Rapper sings and raps on "Best Life," which finds Cardi in a mystical mood as she attributes her success to prayers and the magic of God. Cardi takes one of her most vulnerable vocal turns on "Be Careful," which features the R&B singer Kehlani. Cardi sings the chorus with unvarnished innocence in a song about infidelity. Other guests on *Invasion of Privacy* include the singer SZA and rappers YG and 21 Savage.

Cardi's critics have accused her of being a lousy lyricist, of using sex to advance her career, and even of being not black enough to be a rapper, due to her light skin and Latina heritage. But on *Invasion of Privacy*, Cardi crushes all doubts about her talents and staying power. The album debuted at the top of the *Billboard* 200, and the hit singles from the album made Cardi the first female artist to chart thirteen singles on the Hot 100 simultaneously.

> "*Invasion of Privacy* is even better than everybody was hoping it would be, a whirlwind tour of Planet Cardi, a place where female warriors reign supreme."[47]
> —Rob Sheffield, music reviewer

Television Turns

Cardi promoted *Invasion of Privacy* with numerous radio and television appearances. And, as usual, her personal life remained very public. When Cardi appeared as a musical guest on the comedy sketch show *Saturday Night Live* in April 2018, viewers could not help noticing the baby bump under her tight white dress. Although Cardi had been denying pregnancy rumors for months, it was now obvious that she and Offset were expecting a baby. After she finished singing "Be Careful," she posted a video

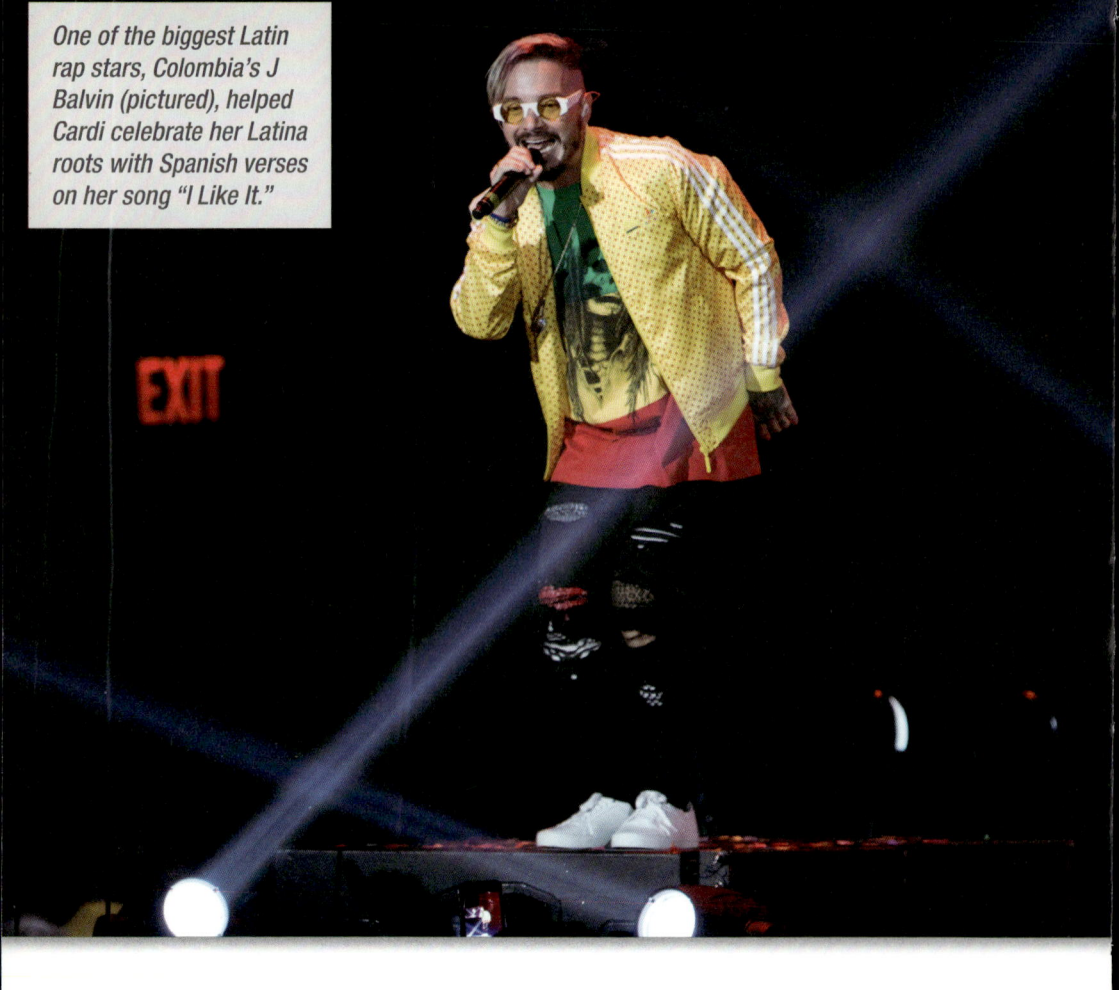

One of the biggest Latin rap stars, Colombia's J Balvin (pictured), helped Cardi celebrate her Latina roots with Spanish verses on her song "I Like It."

on Instagram taken backstage. As friends and family cheered, Cardi raised her arms and expressed joy that she no longer felt obligated to keep her pregnancy secret: "I'm finally free."[48]

Cardi followed her *Saturday Night Live* reveal with a hilarious turn as cohost on the *Tonight Show Starring Jimmy Fallon*. As the first ever cohost of the show, Cardi proved she had stand-up comedy skills while sharing the opening monologue with Fallon. Cardi's sense of comedic timing served her well as she sat behind the host desk with Fallon cracking up the audience and guests with improvised lines. She made several jokes about her pregnancy, and Fallon gave her a baby gift: a baby-sized leopard-print coat like the one she often wears.

On July 11, 2018, Cardi announced the birth of her daughter, Kulture Kiari Cephus, on Instagram. (Offset's real name is Kiari

Kendrell Cephus, and fans speculate the baby's first name might be a reference to Migos's 2017 album, *Culture*.) The Instagram post was accompanied by a photo of a very pregnant Cardi nude and surrounded by flowers.

Cardi B vs. Nicki Minaj

Having a baby did not seem to slow Cardi down, nor did it stop her from getting into very public feuds with famous rappers and even average citizens. A little more than a month after giving birth, Cardi targeted a bartender named Jade and her sister Baddie Gi, who both worked at the Angels Strip Club in Queens, New York. Cardi believed Jade was having an affair with Offset. Jade said that Cardi had been threatening her on Instagram for several months. The beef turned into a physical altercation that ended with Cardi being charged for assault and other crimes.

The strip club brawl attracted media attention—but not nearly as much attention as Cardi's rap beef with Nicki Minaj. The two women have different rap styles—whereas Cardi is a trap rapper, Minaj is more of a pop rapper. But their careers have many parallels, and they are often compared to one another. Both have roots in the Caribbean. Both rappers are short, have breast and butt enhancements, and favor crazy wigs. Cardi and Minaj are often referred to as "queens" by fans, and they have both broken many music industry sales records. The two often complain that the media loves to pit women against one another, but both have had high-profile beefs with other female performers. And the long-running feud between Cardi and Minaj was not made up by fans—it played out very publicly on Twitter and Instagram and even made mainstream media headlines on occasion.

The rap feud began to sizzle after "Bodak Yellow" hit the top of the charts. Cardi and Minaj began throwing snarky bars at each other in their songs. For example, when Minaj teamed up with Katy Perry on the track "Swish Swish," she dropped a line about Offset. The reference was repeated by Minaj in an Instagram post: "Silly rap beefs just get me more checks. My life is a movie, I'm never off set. Me & my aMIGOS No not OFFSET. swish swish awww I got them upset!"[49] Cardi was not happy that Minaj name-checked her man and reacted to the taunt on Instagram. Without mentioning any names, she said that she was happier when she lived in the Bronx because she could punch her detractors in the mouth and not get in trouble. She also wrote that her heart was broken because one of her idols had become a rival.

The Cardi-Minaj rap feud boiled over in September 2018 when both women attended the *Harper's Bazaar* Fashion Week party in New York City. The two rappers met briefly before engaging in a heated verbal exchange. Viral videos show Cardi lunging at Minaj and throwing a shoe at her. Security personnel pinned the fight on Cardi, who was escorted out of the event—barefoot and with a bump on her head. Several hours after the altercation, Cardi posted an Instagram message. She said Minaj had questioned her mothering skills and made inappropriate comments about Kulture: "I let you sneak diss me, I let you lie on me, I let you attempt to stop [me from making money]. . . . You've threatened other artists in the industry, told them if they work with me you'll stop [recording] with them! . . . But when you mention my child, you choose to [make] comments about my abilities to take care of my daughter then all bets are . . . off!!!"[50]

Minaj later denied saying anything about Kulture and called the altercation mortifying. But Minaj kept the rap beef alive on her *Queen Radio* show on iTunes. During one episode, Minaj spent the entire hour dissing Cardi and even featured a guest who said she was harassed by the rapper. After the show, someone leaked Cardi's personal cell phone number to Minaj's fans. Cardi blamed Minaj in an eight-minute video posted on Instagram. In the tirade, Cardi refutes Minaj's insults while bragging about her music sales. Someone from Cardi's camp leaked Minaj's personal phone number online, and the feud continued with no end in sight.

With a visible injury above her eyebrow, Cardi is escorted out of the Harper's Bazaar *Fashion Week party in New York City in 2018. Cardi had been in a physical altercation with rapper Nicki Minaj.*

Making Hits, Breaking Records

The epic rap battle kept Cardi's name trending on social media even as she continued to break records for her music. In October, Cardi collaborated with Maroon 5 on the pop song "Girls Like You." The video, which features a rap break written and performed by Cardi, received more than 2.2 billion views on YouTube, making it the most viewed video of 2018. When "Girls Like You" topped the Hot 100, it extended Cardi's record as the female rapper with the most number-one hits. And after "Girls Like You" replaced Cardi's "I Like It" at number one, she became the first female rapper to replace herself in the top spot. Around the same time, all thirteen tracks on *Invasion of Privacy* were certified gold, meaning they had achieved sales of over 1 million copies. This made Cardi the first female artist to have million-selling hits from every song on an album.

Cardi continued her winning streak with a guest appearance on French rapper DJ Snake's single "Taki Taki." The song, which also features singers Selena Gomez and Ozuna, is in Spanish. "Taki Taki" hit number twenty-seven on the Hot 100 but was a number-one hit in many Spanish-speaking nations, including Argentina, Bolivia, Panama, the Dominican Republic, and Spain. The video, which features Cardi rapping in Spanish, racked up over 1 billion views on YouTube. With the success of "Taki Taki," the Spanish-language magazine *People en Español* named Cardi its Star of the Year for 2018. In an interview with the magazine, Cardi spoke at length about raising a baby. She said she hoped Kulture would grow up to be humble and sharing, and she wanted her to learn at least four languages: Spanish, English, French, and Italian. Cardi also said that being a mom was her proudest and happiest achievement. "When you're famous, so many things are being thrown at you—so much gossip, so many problems, so many beefs, so much money, so much of everything—it just kind of drives you crazy. And then when I see my daughter, it's like a peace of mind."[51]

The Star of the Year honor was one of many Cardi collected as 2018 drew to a close. *Hollywood Reporter* called Cardi "Hip-Hop's current reigning queen."[52] *Entertainment Weekly* listed Cardi as one of its Entertainers of the Year. *Time* magazine included Cardi on its annual list of the one hundred most influential people in the world. *Esquire*, *Vibe*, *Uproxx*, *Spin*, and *People* were among the publications that included *Invasion of Privacy* in their top-ten album lists of 2018. *Rolling Stone*, *Time*, and *Entertainment Tonight* called *Invasion of Privacy* the best album of the year. The *New York Times* said the record was one of the best debuts of the millennium.

> "When you're famous, so many things are being thrown at you—so much gossip, so many problems, so many beefs, so much money . . . it just kind of drives you crazy."[51]
>
> —Cardi B

Cardi's Strip Club Melee

In 2018 Cardi B sent threatening messages on Instagram to a bartender named Jade, who worked at Angels Strip Club in Queens, New York. Cardi believed her husband, Offset, was having an affair with Jade. According to media reports, Jade was working with her sister, known as Baddie Gi, on August 15, 2018, when Cardi arrived with her bodyguards and other members of her entourage. The sisters allege that Cardi watched as her posse attacked them, pulling their hair, punching them, and hitting one of them with a large ashtray.

When Offset's rap trio, Migos, played at the strip club two weeks later, Cardi was there again with her posse. According to a report by NBC News, a surveillance video shows Cardi hurling an ice bucket while other members of her group threw bottles and chairs at Jade and Baddie Gi.

Several months after the altercations, a lawyer for Jade and Baddie Gi filed a police report. Cardi was arrested in October and was later charged with two felony counts of attempted assault with intent to cause serious physical injury. If found guilty, Cardi could be sentenced to four years in prison. As of fall 2019, a trial date had not been set.

Cardi was fifth on *Billboard*'s Year-End Top Artists chart, and *Invasion of Privacy* ranked sixth in total album sales. The album was listed as the most-streamed album by a female artist on Apple Music and on Spotify. Cardi received twelve nominations at the 2018 MTV Video Music Awards—more than any other artist. She won three of those awards, including Best New Artist and Song of the Summer for "I Like It." *Invasion of Privacy* won the award for Album of the Year at the BET Hip Hop Awards, and Cardi was the first woman to win the Best Rap Album award at the sixty-first annual Grammy Awards.

After Cardi won the Grammy in February 2019, she was targeted by online trolls, forcing her to deactivate her Instagram account. She managed to stay offline for only three days. Cardi jokingly said she was back from retirement with an Instagram post announcing her new single with Bruno Mars. The song, "Please Me," was Cardi's first release since *Invasion of Privacy,* and it hit big. Dominated by Cardi's raps, the song debuted at number five on the Hot 100 and racked up nearly 28 million streams.

Cardi accepts the Best Rap Album award at the 61st annual Grammy Awards in 2019. She was the first woman to win the award.

Big and Little Screens

Like many successful rappers, Cardi decided to take on an acting role. In September 2019, she appeared in the film *Hustlers* with Jennifer Lopez, Constance Wu, and Julia Stiles. The movie, set in New York City in 2008, is about strippers who scam rich customers out of thousands of dollars. Not surprisingly, Cardi plays a stripper in the film, but she felt her performance was limited because she was still recovering from recent liposuction and breast augmentation surgery. However, Cardi had praise for Lopez, who took grueling dance lessons to take on the stripper role: "[Lopez] said she was training, I see it now, because everybody thinks it's so easy to do. No it ain't. You can't do it at home."[53]

Cardi also had plans to return to the small screen, signing up to be a judge alongside Chance the Rapper on a ten-part talent search show called *Rhythm + Flow*. The program, slated to debut on Netflix in October 2019, was the first hip-hop competition on television.

Cardi and Bernie

As a performer and a personality, Cardi always astonishes her fans, but many were probably surprised when she entered the realm of politics. In January 2019, when the US government shut down over disagreements between President Donald Trump and Congress, Cardi took to Instagram to criticize the president in her unique, quirky, profanity-laced style. The post generated over 4 million likes.

In August, with the primary season already well under way, twenty-six-year-old Cardi sat down to interview seventy-seven-year-old Democratic senator Bernie Sanders, whom she once nicknamed "Daddy Bernie." Sanders was one of a group of candidates seeking the Democratic nomination for president. Cardi is a Sanders supporter, and she has urged her fans to vote for him. As the two talked in a Detroit nail salon, Cardi asked questions previously solicited from fans on social media. She sought Sanders's views on topics ranging from health care to police brutality.

In a thoughtful twelve-minute discussion, Cardi and Sanders delved into serious issues facing many Americans. She described the problems some of her fans faced when dealing with immigration officials and the police. And she drew on her own experience to explain why she thought the minimum wage should be raised: "As a New Yorker, not now, but you know,

> ### Cardi B Interviews Bernie Sanders
>
> Cardi B delved into politics in 2019 when she interviewed Democratic senator Bernie Sanders, who was seeking the Democratic nomination for president. Excerpts from the interview follow:
>
> [Cardi:] "Don't you ever feel scared that these people who run drug companies, and these schools, you know it's all a business, are you scared that you'll get so many powerful people upset?". . .
>
> [Sanders:] "Cardi, that's what I've been doing my whole life.". . .
>
> [Cardi, discussing police brutality:] "That is discouraging our people, it's discouraging us to fight. It makes us feel like we're worthless. We constantly see our men getting killed every day. And it seems like nobody cares, nobody's sympathizing, nobody's talking about it."
>
> [Sanders:] "If a police officer kills somebody, that killing must be investigated by the United States Department of Justice. We at the federal level must make sure we do everything we can to make sure that police departments look like the communities that they serve, not like an oppressive army. . . . Young people have got to get involved in the political process. Register to vote. It is not hard. It takes you five minutes. Register to vote."
>
> Quoted in Luke Darby, "Cardi B Asks Bernie Sanders If He's 'Scared' of Upsetting Many Powerful People," *GQ*, August 15, 2019. www.gq.com/story/cardi-b-bernie-sanders-interview.

when I was not famous, I just felt like no matter how many jobs I got, I wasn't able to make ends meet. Like, I wasn't able to pay my rent, get transportation and eat."[54] Sanders promised to more than double the national minimum wage from $7.25 an hour to $15 an hour if elected.

The interview with Sanders showed that Cardi could step away from her role as a braggadocious, X-rated rapper. Speaking as a mother concerned about her child's future, Cardi revealed a considerate, intellectual side that her trap rap fans rarely see. But Cardi has always been a complex character. She can be nasty and compassionate, joyous and negative, generous and greedy—all in a single rap song. And that might be the key to Cardi's success. Although few people have followed similar career paths, Cardi continues to come across as a "regular, degular, shmegular girl" who just happens to be one of the world's most successful female rappers.

Introduction: Empowered and Empowering

1. Vanessa Grigoriadis, "Cardi B and Offset: A Hip-Hop Love Story," *Rolling Stone*, June 20, 2018. www.rollingstone.com.
2. Quoted in Diane Soloway, "Cardi B Gets Candid: Hip-Hop's Fiercest Female Rapper Speaks Out About Her Past, Her Career, and Being a New Mom," *W Magazine*, October 9, 2018. www.wmagazine.com.
3. Quoted in Ashley Iasimone, "Cardi B on Being a Feminist: 'Anything a Man Can Do, I Can Do,'" *Billboard*, February 11, 2018. www.billboard.com.
4. Quoted in Caity Weaver, "Cardi B's Money Moves," *GQ*, April 9, 2018. www.gq.com.

Chapter One: Born in the Bronx

5. Quoted in Thatiana Diaz, "Cardi B Reveals the Meaning of Her Name and Promises to Be a Better Role Model," *People*, November 6, 2017. https://people.com.
6. Quoted in "Cardi B and 'Sounding Uneducated,'" Ace Linguist, December 4, 2018. www.acelinguist.com.
7. Quoted in Rawiya Kameir, "Cardi B's So-Called Life," *Fader*, February 29, 2016. www.thefader.com.
8. Quoted in Weaver, "Cardi B's Money Moves."
9. Quoted in Weaver, "Cardi B's Money Moves."
10. Quoted in Soloway, "Cardi B Gets Candid."
11. Quoted in Soloway, "Cardi B Gets Candid."
12. Quoted in Marjua Estevez, "Cardi B Doesn't Give a F**k, and Neither Should You," Vibe, November 16, 2016. www.vibe.com.
13. Quoted in Iasimone, "Cardi B on Being a Feminist."
14. Quoted in Weaver, "Cardi B's Money Moves."
15. Quoted in Estevez, "Cardi B Doesn't Give a F**k, and Neither Should You."

Chapter Two: Building a Following

16. Quoted in Kameir, "Cardi B's So-Called Life."
17. Angie Liu, "How Cardi B Used Social Media to Take Over the World," Medium, May 23, 2018. https://medium.com.

18. Quoted in Clover Hope, "America Loves Cardi B, *Love & Hip-Hop*'s Best New Cast Member," Jezebel, January 5, 2016. https://themuse.jezebel.com.
19. Quoted in Kameir, "Cardi B's So-Called Life."
20. Quoted in Rachel Torgerson, "Why Cardi B Won't Ever Wear Certain Designers," *Cosmopolitan*, December 14, 2017. www.cosmopolitan.com.
21. Liu, "How Cardi B Used Social Media to Take Over the World."
22. Quoted in Weaver, "Cardi B's Money Moves."
23. Hope, "America Loves Cardi B, *Love & Hip-Hop's* Best New Cast Member."
24. Quoted in Kameir, "Cardi B's So-Called Life."
25. Quoted in Kameir, "Cardi B's So-Called Life."
26. Quoted in Kevin Jackson, "Cardi B's Caribbean Connection," *Jamaica Observer*, September 28, 2017. http://m.jamaicaobserver.com.
27. Quoted in Weaver, "Cardi B's Money Moves."
28. Quoted in Estevez, "Cardi B Doesn't Give a F**k, and Neither Should You."
29. Craig Jenkins, "Cardi B's 'Gangsta Bitch Music Vol. 1' Is the First Good Record to Come Out of 'Love and Hip-Hop,'" Vice, March 9, 2016. www.vice.com.
30. Quoted in Lara Elmayan, "Public Image: Cardi B," MAC Cosmetics, April 27, 2017. https://m.maccosmetics.com.
31. Liu, "How Cardi B Used Social Media to Take Over the World."

Chapter Three: The Hottest Thing in Hip-Hop

32. Quoted in Theo Wenner, "Migos: High Times and Heartache with the Three Kings of Hip-Hop," *Rolling Stone*, January 23, 2018. www.rollingstone.com.
33. Quoted in Rawiya Kameir, "Cardi B Did It Her Way," *Fader*, June 22, 2017. www.thefader.com.
34. Quoted in Emina Lukarcanin, "Cardi B and Offset's Relationship: A Timeline," *Billboard*, December 5, 2018. www.billboard.com.
35. Quoted in Lukarcanin, "Cardi B and Offset's Relationship."
36. Quoted in Lukarcanin, "Cardi B and Offset's Relationship."

37. Quoted in KC Orcutt, "Cardi B's Reaction to Being Nominated for a BET Award Is Too Cute," BET, May 15, 2017. www.bet.com.
38. Aaron Williams, "No Offense to Remy Ma but Cardi B Was Robbed at the BET Awards," Uproxx, June 26, 2017. https://uproxx.com.
39. Quoted in Alyssa Norwin, "Cardi B Fears Winning BET Award over 'Idol' Remy Ma: It Would Be 'Awkward,'" Hollywood Life, June 22, 2017. https://hollywoodlife.com.
40. Brittany Spanos, "The Year of Cardi B," *Rolling Stone*, October 30, 2017. www.rollingstone.com.
41. Quoted in Spanos, "The Year of Cardi B."
42. Quoted in Grigoriadis, "Cardi B and Offset: A Hip-Hop Love Story."
43. Tom Breihan, "Cardi B Is a Great Rapper, and You Need to Start Taking Her Seriously," Stereogum, July 19, 2017. www.stereogum.com.
44. Quoted in Brian Anthony Hernandez, "Sneak Peek at G-Eazy's Next Album: Chet Backer Sample, Halsey Duet, Cardi B Collab," Fuse, September 2, 2017. www.fuse.tv.
45. Sheldon Pearce, "'Bartier Cardi,'" *Pitchfork*, December 22, 2017. https://pitchfork.com.

Chapter Four: Hip-Hop's Reigning Queen

46. Quoted in Chelsea Stewart, "Celebs Who Can't Stand Cardi B," Nicki Swift, 2019. www.nickiswift.com.
47. Rob Sheffield, "Review: Cardi B's Debut 'Invasion of Privacy,' Is Personal and Undeniable," *Rolling Stone*, April 6, 2018. www.rollingstone.com.
48. Quoted in Joanne Kavanagh, "Bump in the Night: Cardi B Announces She Is Pregnant by Debuting Her Baby Bump on *Saturday Night Live*," *Sun*, April 8, 2018. www.thesun.co.uk.
49. Quoted in Nerisha Penrose, "A Timeline of Nicki Minaj & Cardi B's Complicated Relationship," *Billboard*, November 1, 2017. www.billboard.com.
50. Quoted in Maia Efrem, "How Long Has This Nicki Minaj & Cardi B Feud Been Going On? Here's a Timeline," Refinery 29, October 30, 2018. www.refinery29.com.

51. Quoted in Suzette Fernandez, "Cardi B Says She Won't Allow Her Baby to Forget Her in 'People en Espanol' Cover Story," *Billboard*, October 30, 2018. www.billboard.com.
52. Quoted in Michael O'Connell, "Cardi B and Chance the Rapper Will Judge Hip-Hop Competition 'Rhythm + Flow' for Netflix," *Hollywood Reporter*, November 12, 2018. www.hollywoodreporter.com.
53. Quoted in Lisa Respers France, "Cardi B Didn't 'Shine' on the Pole in 'Hustlers' and Here's Why," CNN, August 26, 2019. www.cnn.com.
54. Quoted in Emily Zemler, "Watch Cardi B Interview Bernie Sanders About Health Care, Minimum Wage, and Immigration," *Rolling Stone*, August 16, 2019. www.rollingstone.com.

Important Events in the Life of Cardi B

1992
Cardi B is born Belcalis Marlenis Almánzar in the Bronx, New York, on October 11.

1995
Cardi B's sister, Hennessy, is born.

1998
Cardi B drops out of high school.

2011
Cardi B begins her career as a stripper.

2013
Cardi B begins posting humorous videos on Instagram.

2014
Cardi B has around 1 million Instagram followers.

2015
Cardi B performs at a strip club for the last time on her twenty-third birthday; she is cast to appear on the reality television show *Love & Hip-Hop: New York*.

2016
Cardi B releases her first mixtape, *Gangsta Bitch Music, Vol. 1*.

2017
Her breakout single "Bodak Yellow (Money Moves)" hits number one on the charts.

2018
Cardi B releases her hit album *Invasion of Privacy*. Cardi B gives birth to a daughter, Kulture Kiari Cephus, on July 11.

2019
Cardi B appears as a judge on the Netflix hip-hop talent search show *Rhythm + Flow*; she interviews senator and Democratic presidential candidate Bernie Sanders.

Books

Judy Dodge Cummings, *Hip-Hop Culture*. Minneapolis: Essential Library, 2017.

Stuart A. Kallen, *Rap and Hip-Hop*. San Diego: ReferencePoint, 2020.

Joe L. Morgan, *Cardi B*. Broomall, PA: Mason Crest, 2018.

New York Times Editorial Staff, *Influential Hip-Hop Artists: Kendrick Lamar, Nicki Minaj, and Others*. New York: *New York Times* Educational, 2018.

Vanessa Oswald, *Hip-Hop: A Cultural and Musical Revolution*. New York: Lucent, 2019.

Internet Sources

Vanessa Grigoriadis, "Cardi B and Offset: A Hip-Hop Love Story," *Rolling Stone*, June 20, 2018. www.rollingstone.com.

Ashley Iasimone, "Cardi B on Being a Feminist: 'Anything a Man Can Do, I Can Do,'" *Billboard*, February 11, 2018. www.billboard.com.

Angie Liu, "How Cardi B Used Social Media to Take Over the World," Medium, May 23, 2018. https://medium.com.

Diane Soloway, "Cardi B Gets Candid: Hip-Hop's Fiercest Female Rapper Speaks Out About Her Past, Her Career, and Being a New Mom," *W Magazine*, October 9, 2018. www.wmagazine.com.

Caity Weaver, "Cardi B's Money Moves," *GQ*, April 9, 2018. www.gq.com.

Note: Boldface page numbers indicate illustrations.

A$AP Rocky, 38
Almánzar, Belcalis Marlenis. *See* Cardi B
Almánzar, Carlos (father), 7
Almánzar, Esperanza (grandmother), 8
Almánzar, Hennessy Carolina (sister), 7, **9**
Angels Strip Club melee, 43, 47

"Bad and Boujee" (song), 30
Baddie Gi, 43, 47
"Bartier Cardi" (song), 39
BET Hip Hop Awards, 33, 39, 47
Beyoncé, 4
Billboard music awards, 4
Bloods (street gang), 12, 13, 31–32
"Bodak Yellow (Money Moves)" (song), 4, 34–37
Borough of Manhattan Community College, 12–13, **14**
Breihan, Tom, 37
Brown, Foxy, 6

Cardi B (Belcalis Marlenis Almánzar), **20**
 accepting Grammy Award, **48**
 in Angels Strip Club melee, 43, 47
 on being a feminist, 6
 birth of, 7
 develops fashion line, 19–21
 early life of, 8–12
 endorsements by, 24, 28
 on fame, 46
 feud with Nicki Minaj, 43–44, **45**
 on gang life, 13
 health problems of, 10–11
 on her mother, 11, 12
 hip-hop debut of, 23–25
 important events in life of, 56
 interviews Bernie Sanders, 49–51
 job as stripper, 13–15, 16–17
 makes rap debut with the Lox, 29–30
 marriage of, 32
 at Music Midtown festival, **5**
 nominated for BET Hip Hop Awards, 33–34
 with Offset, **31**
 with sister, **9**

58

social media following, 5, 18–19
takes on acting role, 49
trap rap style of, 27, 39, 43
undergoes surgical enhancements, 15–16
wins BET Best Featured Verse award, 39
Cephus, Kiari Kendrell. *See* Offset
Cephus, Kulture Kiari (daughter), 4, 42–43
   Cardi-Minaj feud and, 44, 46
Chance the Rapper, 33–34, 41, 49
"Cheap Ass Weave" (song), 25
Coldest Winter Ever, The (Sister Souljah), 11–12, 16
Combs, Sean "Diddy," 29
Culture II, 39
Cupcakke, 33

DJ Self, 26
Drake, 29

Entertainment Weekly (magazine), 46

Fader (magazine), 31
Fallon, Jimmy, 42
Fashion Nova, 19–**20**, 24
Filthy America . . . It's Beautiful (album), 29

"Foreva" (song), 26
Gangsta Bitch Music, Vol. 1 (mixtape), 27–28
Gangsta Bitch Music, Vol. 2 (mixtape), 28
G-Eazy, 38, 39
"Girls Like You" (song), 45
Gomez, Selena, 46
GQ (magazine), 13
Grammy Awards, 47, **48**
Grigoriadis, Vanessa, 4

Harper's Bazaar Fashion Week party, 44
Hill, Lauryn, 37
Hip-Hop Squares (TV program), 33
Hollywood Life (website), 34
Hollywood Reporter (magazine), 46
Hustlers (film), 49

i-D (magazine), 33
Invasion of Privacy (album), 40–41
   awards won by, 4, 47
   included in top-ten album lists, 46
"It's All About the Benjamins" (song), 30

Jade, 43, 47
Jenkins, Craig, 26–27

Kallman, Craig, 5
Kash Doll, 33
Katie Got Bandz, 33
Kodak Black, 34, **35,** 36

Lady Leshurr, 25
Lil' Kim, 6, 30
Liu, Angie, 18, 21, 28
Lopez, Jennifer, 49
Love & Hip-Hop (TV program), 21–22, 26, 27, 28
the Lox (hip-hop group), 29–30

Maroon 5, 45
Mars, Bruno, 48
Met Gala, 30
Migos (hip-hop trio), 30, 32, 39, 40, 47
Minaj, Nicki, 4, 6, 29, 34, 39
  feud with Cardi, 43–44
"MotorSport" (song), 39
MTV Video Music Awards, 47

New York Times (newspaper), 46
"No Flockin" (song), 34, 36

Offset (Kiari Kendrell Cephus), 30–31, **31,** 32, 33, 42–43
Ozuna, 46

Painting Pictures (album), 36

Pearce, Sheldon, 39
People en Español (magazine), 46
Pitchfork (magazine), 37
Playtime Is Over (mixtape), 34
"Please Me" (song), 48

"Queen's Speech 4" (song), 25

Remy Ma, 22, **23,** 30, 33–34
Rhythm + Flow (TV program), 49

Sanders, Bernie, 49–51
Saturday Night Live (TV program), 41–42
"Sauce Boyz" (song), 26
Shaggy, 25, **25**
Sheffield, Rob, 40
Sister Souljah, 11–12, 16
social media influencers, 18
South Bronx, 8, **10**
Stiles, Julia, 49
"Stir Fry" (song), 30
Swift, Taylor, 37, **38**
"Swish Swish" (song), 43–44

"Taki Taki" (song), 46
That's So Raven (TV program), 11

60

360 Degrees of Power
   (album), 16
Time (magazine), 46
*Tonight Show Starring Jimmy
   Fallon* (TV program), 42
trap rap, 27, 34–35

Trump, Donald, 49
"Two Birds, One Stone"
   (song), 29

Williams, Aaron, 34
Wu, Constance, 49

Cover: lev radin

- 5: Associated Press
- 9: Associated Press
- 10: Associated Press
- 14: littlenySTOCK/Shutterstock
- 20: Associated Press
- 23: Everett Collection/Newscom
- 25: Dafydd Owen/Retna/Avalon.red/Newscom
- 31: RB/Bauergriffin/MEGA/Newscom
- 35: ZOJ/JLN Photography/WENN/Newscom
- 38: JStone/Shutterstock
- 42: Alberto E. Tamargo/Sipa USA/Newscom
- 45: Associated Press
- 48: Mike Blake/Reuters/Newscom

PICTURE CREDITS

ABOUT THE AUTHOR

Stuart A. Kallen is the author of more than 350 nonfiction books for children and young adults. He has written on topics ranging from the theory of relativity to the art of electronic dance music. In 2018 Kallen won a Green Earth Book Award from the Nature Generation environmental organization for his book *Trashing the Planet: Examining the Global Garbage Glut*. In his spare time he is a singer, songwriter, and guitarist in San Diego.

JUN 19 2020

HEWLETT-WOODMERE PUBLIC LIBRARY

3 1327 00684 8311

28 DAY LOAN

Hewlett-Woodmere Public Library
Hewlett, New York 11557

Business Phone 516-374-1967
Recorded Announcements 516-374-1667
Website www.hwpl.org